Rapunzel

A Day to Remember

DISNEY
PRINCESS

Printed in the United States of America
First Edition
3 5 7 9 10 8 6 4
G658-7729-4 14183
ISBN 978-1-4231-4176-1

For more Disney Press fun, visit www.disneybooks.com

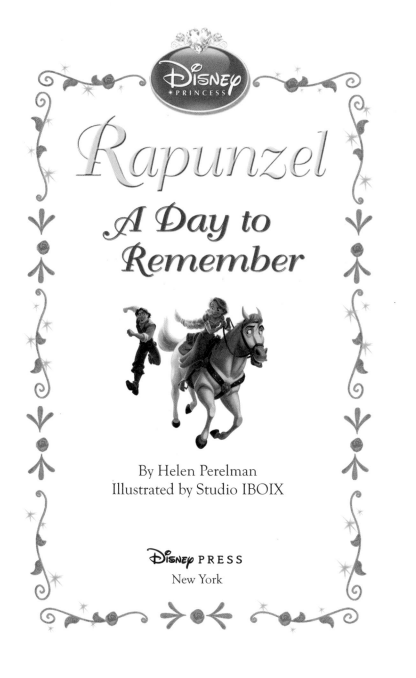

Rapunzel
A Day to Remember

By Helen Perelman
Illustrated by Studio IBOIX

DISNEP PRESS

New York

Chapter One

Rapunzel sighed happily as she walked through a charming village. Her very, very, very, very, very, very, very long golden hair shone in the bright sunlight. A few village girls had woven Rapunzel's long locks into a thick braid. With her hair up and out of the way, Rapunzel was free to explore the town. Her chameleon, Pascal, a thief named Flynn Rider, and Maximus, a royal guard horse, were by her side.

Rapunzel swung her arms out wide and twirled in a circle. It was wonderful to be out walking. She was used to spending her days in a tower. She had lived in one for nearly eighteen years with only Mother Gothel and Pascal. Mother Gothel had always told her it was too dangerous to go outside the tower and had never let her leave.

So Rapunzel had decided to sneak away while Mother Gothel was gone.

"I love this town!" she cried. "There are so many people. They seem happy and helpful, not mean." She looked around, taking in the scene. "Mother Gothel was definitely wrong about this place. She is always telling me people in town aren't so kind."

Pascal held on tightly to Rapunzel's shoulder as she spun around. If it were up to him, he and Rapunzel would still be in the tower. He was feeling a little unsure about all this adventure and about being far from home.

"You really don't get out much, do you?" Flynn asked. He raised one of his dark eyebrows and grinned.

"No," Rapunzel replied. Her green eyes were wide with excitement. "I don't."

Her plan to leave the tower for a couple of days was turning out even better than she'd imagined. Even though Mother Gothel had warned her about Flynn, Rapunzel felt that she could trust him.

She glanced at Flynn, who was looking

over his shoulder. There were WANTED signs with his picture posted all over the kingdom. He had to be careful. He was wanted for his latest heist—stealing a jeweled royal crown.

This was not the best place for him to be strolling about, but he had made a deal with Rapunzel. He'd shown up at her tower, and she'd captured him. He thought he could charm her, but Rapunzel didn't care about his good looks or his dazzling smile. At least, he liked to think it was dazzling.

Instead, Rapunzel had hidden the stolen crown and demanded he take her to see the floating lanterns that appeared in the night sky every year on her birthday.

If Rapunzel was true to her word, he would

soon have the crown back. Flynn watched Rapunzel dancing in the street with some of the villagers. Not a bad bargain, he thought. Though he could have done without the frying pan to his head upon arriving at the tower.

And now Rapunzel was exploring the village near the palace. She turned and saw Maximus bringing up the rear. "Come on, Max," she said, urging the horse on. "I bet I can find you a carrot around here."

Maximus's ears twitched. He wasn't sure how he had gotten himself involved with this village tour, but a snack sounded good to him. He neighed happily.

Maximus had been doing his royal duty, chasing Flynn and the stolen crown. Then he'd met Rapunzel. She told him that every year on her birthday, she'd watch the sky from her tower and wonder about the lanterns. Her only dream was to see the lanterns and find out what they were all about.

"I can't believe how many stores there are," Rapunzel said. She ran along sidewalks decorated with royal purple flags. "There's a pastry store, a clothing store, and, oh, look at this!" She raced across the street. "A whole store for books!"

Flynn nodded. "It's a village," he said, rolling his eyes. "Villages are usually full of stores.

"Is there something that you want to buy?" he asked Rapunzel. They had some free time before that night. "Maybe you'd

like to go into one of these stores?"

"Hmmm," Rapunzel said. The music stopped, and she tapped her finger on her chin. She had never actually gone shopping before. Every once in a while Mother Gothel had gotten her new clothes, a book, or paints, but Rapunzel had never been inside a store. She hadn't even imagined going into a store by herself to pick out what she wanted! Oh, what should she get? A new dress? Food? Books? If only Mother Gothel could see her now!

A man was standing next to a vegetable cart on the corner. On top of the cart was a large bunch of carrots. When the man saw Rapunzel, he sprang into action.

"Would you like some fresh vegetables?"

he asked kindly. "They are from my farm outside the village." He smiled. He had not sold anything all day and was getting anxious. "Best produce in town," he said with a wink.

Rapunzel was surprised that this man would ask her if she wanted vegetables. She blushed. "You are so kind," she said. She pointed to the carrots. "I think my friend Maximus would love a carrot. Thank you."

The man nodded and handed Rapunzel a carrot. "Here you are, milady," he said.

"Thank you, kind sir," Rapunzel replied. She took the carrot and turned to give it to Maximus.

The horse gobbled up the treat, impressed that Rapunzel was true to her word. Even though he hadn't known her for long, he'd liked her from the start.

"When I make a promise, I never break it," Rapunzel told the horse. She scratched his long nose. Then Rapunzel kept walking. She didn't realize she had to pay for the carrots! She'd thought that the farmer was just being nice.

Flynn saw that the man's friendly smile had given way to a frown. He wanted his money.

Maximus glared at Flynn. He knew that Flynn was a thief, and he didn't want any stealing on his watch.

Noticing the horse's reaction, Flynn decided he'd have to pay for the carrot himself. He flipped some coins to the man without Rapunzel seeing.

When Flynn caught up with her, she smiled at him. "I knew Mother Gothel was wrong about people. That man was so nice to give Maximus a carrot!"

Flynn grinned. "Yes, it was very big of him." *That girl really has spent a lot of* time alone in the tower, he thought.

"There's so much to explore!" Rapunzel said, running ahead. "Come on, let's see what's around the corner."

Looking over at Maximus, Flynn raised an eyebrow. He'd never known anyone who found walking through town so exciting.

Pascal noticed and turned red. That Flynn was no good.

Chapter Two

*R*apunzel stood in front of an art gallery with her mouth hanging open. She couldn't believe the paintings hanging in the window. Each one was more colorful than the next. There were waterfalls, beach scenes, and majestic mountains, all in thick gold frames.

Flynn put his hand under her chin, gently pushing her jaw closed. "You don't want a fly to get caught in there, Blondie."

"Oh," Rapunzel said. "But just look at all these paintings!" She motioned for Max and Pascal to come over.

Then she turned to Flynn. "Let's go in," she said, grabbing hold of the door.

Before Flynn could answer, Rapunzel was inside the shop. The thief looked over at Maximus. The horse narrowed his eyes. He wanted Flynn to know he shouldn't make a run for it.

"We'll be out soon," Flynn promised, smiling.

Maximus peered in. The large window would make keeping an eye on Flynn and Rapunzel easy. He swished his tail and stood guard.

Inside the shop, Rapunzel could smell

fresh paint. "An artist must be at work." She walked slowly around the room. "This art is wonderful."

"Hello?" a voice called. "May I help you?" A short man with bushy black hair came out from behind a curtain. He was wearing a blue smock that was splattered with paint. In one hand he held a colorful palette and in the other a paintbrush.

Rapunzel turned around. Her long, thick braid knocked down a painting. Luckily, Flynn was standing nearby and caught the canvas.

"Hello," Rapunzel said boldly, walking toward the painter. "I am Rapunzel. And this is my . . . uh, well . . . it's Flynn Rider and my friend Pascal. We were just walking by and had to come in to see these paintings. Are you the artist?"

The short, round man blushed. "Oh, well, I'm . . . thank you," he stammered. "I'm so glad that you came in."

"Are all of these paintings yours?" Rapunzel asked. Her green eyes sparkled as she looked at the artwork. "There must be hundreds."

The man grinned. "Actually, there are more in the back room." He pointed to the dark curtain behind them. Then he reached a hand out to Rapunzel. "My name is Roberto."

"I'm so happy to meet you," Rapunzel said, shaking his hand. "I've never met another artist."

Roberto laughed. "Ah, so are you an artist as well?"

"Yes."

"And what about you?" Roberto asked Flynn.

"Oh, I'm not an artist," Flynn said, flashing what he thought was an award-winning smile. "I'll be the model." He peered into a mirror hanging on the wall and checked his hair. "I'm known for my good looks." He struck a pose with his hands on his hips and his chest puffed out.

"You are?" Rapunzel asked.

Flynn slicked back his brown hair. He ignored Rapunzel's comment. "Though no one seems to get my nose quite right," he mumbled disappointedly.

Pascal jumped to Flynn's shoulder and flashed a big grin. If Rapunzel was going to paint anyone, it should be him!

Rapunzel did not notice Pascal posing. She was too distracted by the back wall of Roberto's shop. Long, thin shelves were piled high with supplies. Two large wooden boxes were filled to the brim with brushes. Rapunzel peered into the box and picked up a fan-shaped brush.

"You're lucky to have so many paints and brushes," Rapunzel said, in awe. "I've never seen so many."

"Yes, I do have a lot," Roberto confessed. "It was my dream to run an art school." He wiped his forehead nervously. "But I didn't get any students, so now I just try to sell my own work."

"An art school?" Rapunzel asked. She tilted her head. She had never heard of such a thing.

"Yes, you know," Roberto said, "so I can teach students about art and painting."

"Wow!" Rapunzel squealed. Her green eyes grew wide. "I never dreamed there was someone who could teach me to be a better painter."

Pascal plopped down on Flynn's shoulder. This was going to be a longer stop than he had thought. Rapunzel definitely had a plan brewing.

"Oh, you are a self-taught artist?" Roberto exclaimed happily.

"Well, she didn't get out much before she met me," Flynn said, sitting down in a chair. He grinned at Rapunzel.

"Well, I still managed to capture you . . . with only my bare hands."

"And seventy feet of hair and a frying pan to my gourd," Flynn retorted.

Rapunzel rolled her eyes. She turned to Roberto. "Please, I don't have much time today, but I'd love to have a lesson."

Roberto scurried around. "Oh, this is wonderful! I would love to give you a free lesson!" He started grabbing tubes of paints and brushes.

Clapping her hands together, Rapunzel gasped. "Really? Oh, how extraordinary! Flynn, Pascal, did you hear? I'm going to have a real art lesson."

"I heard," Flynn said. "And are you going to paint me?" He gave her a wide, toothy grin.

"Maybe," Rapunzel said mischievously.

"Isn't this exciting?" Rapunzel said to Pascal. "Getting painting tips from a real

painter like Roberto is going to be fantastic."

"Let me get some canvases," Roberto told her. "I've never had such an interested student before!" And in a flash, he had disappeared behind the curtain.

Rapunzel faced Flynn. "I knew this place was special. Thank you for bringing me here today."

Flynn smiled and nodded. He was ready to take full credit for this stop—especially since it was making Rapunzel so happy. To him, she was a mystery as big as that thick braid on her head. Luckily the day was turning out better than he had expected.

Chapter Three

Roberto raced around the shop, grabbing paints and brushes. "Oh, this will be a perfect class," he mumbled to himself. "The weather is just right. The blue sky, the green trees . . . this is all very good."

"Excuse me, Roberto," Rapunzel asked. "May I help you?"

Roberto stopped moving. He had a pile of canvases on his head, and his hands were full of paint tubes and brushes.

"Yes, thank you," he said. He handed her the brushes. "There's a wooden box under the cabinet. Could you put these brushes in that? This way we can carry all we need out to the meadow."

"An art lesson outdoors?" Rapunzel said with a smile. She carefully placed the brushes in the box. "Flynn, what could be more perfect?"

Flynn was half asleep in Roberto's chair, his hair flopped over his eyes. Pascal stuck out his tongue, zapping Flynn on the nose. Flynn jolted awake. "I heard you," he snapped. "I'm just trying to get a little beauty rest before my portrait."

The chameleon flared his nostrils. Didn't

Flynn know that Rapunzel was going to paint Pascal? After all, he'd been her best friend for years. He hadn't just come on the scene . . . like some people.

"Well, we'll see," Rapunzel said to Flynn. "It depends how I feel when I get to the meadow." She scooped up Pascal. "No more dim tower light! I can't wait to feel the sunshine on my face as I paint."

Roberto stopped what he was doing and stared at her. "You've never painted outside? Oh, my dear, you will love the way the light plays upon the meadow. It is magnificent! And this is the best time of day. You'll see." He tied the canvases together with a cord. "What do you enjoy painting?"

"Mostly suns," Rapunzel told him. She thought of her tower home and how she had decorated the ceiling with the sun. "I've never painted anything fancy like you." She waved to the many paintings around the shop.

"Oh, I've done lots of different subjects," Roberto said. "Come, let me show you my private collection." He led Rapunzel, Flynn, and Pascal to the back room.

"Each of these piles is from a different place," Roberto explained. "I traveled all over the world before settling in this village."

Flynn flipped through a stack of paintings. He pulled out one of an Egyptian pyramid. "You were in the desert?"

Roberto leaned back on a stool. "Yes. Oh, that was a lovely trip," he said, "but those pyramids took a while to paint."

"Let alone build," Flynn said, laughing.

Rapunzel leaned in closer to the painting Flynn was holding. "I love the detail. You have such a steady hand."

Roberto waved his arm. "Oh, that's just technique. I can show you how to do that."

A painting of a bright blue sea caught Rapunzel's eye. "Where is this place?" she inquired. The boats on the sea were colorful, and the seaport was filled with people.

"That is my home in Italy," Roberto said. "It is a fishing village. I was standing up on the hill outside my house."

"Now that's a cliff I would not want to jump off," Flynn added. He pointed to the big drop down to the sea.

"Yes," Roberto told him. "There are many high cliffs—a good opportunity for a bird's-eye view."

"I know all about that," Rapunzel muttered. Many of her paintings at home were from a bird's-eye view! As she gazed at Roberto's seaside painting she couldn't help being amazed. This was a real place, not just a picture in a book. "Oh, I'd love to travel like Roberto," she said with a sigh.

"One adventure day at a time, Blondie," Flynn said.

Rapunzel didn't respond. She was watching Roberto stare at the painting. "You miss your home, don't you?"

"I do," Roberto said with a heavy sigh. "I don't have the money to go back there," he told her. "Maybe someday I will be able to visit—and to paint."

Pascal jumped up to a small table where a colorful painting was displayed. He posed dramatically in front of the painting, changing colors every few steps.

"Oh, Pascal," Rapunzel said, laughing.

"You are a master of color." She picked him up. "And a master of disguises!"

She looked at the painting that Pascal stood in front of. "And what foreign land is this?" In the painting, a bright blue river ran through a field filled with dozens of colorful blossoms. Rapunzel could almost smell the flowers and feel bright sunshine on her face.

"That is the meadow I want to take you to," Roberto said. "I told you that of all the places I have traveled, this kingdom has the most beautiful landscapes."

Pascal jumped in front of the painting again. This time his skin changed to every color of the rainbow at the same time. He looked like a beautiful bouquet.

"Extraordinary!" Roberto sang out.

"A true show-off," Rapunzel said, picking up her pet. She gave him a kiss on the nose.

Flynn peered out the window. "We should get going," he said. "You'll want to have time to get my portrait just right."

Rapunzel laughed. "Don't worry, I'll paint you a special keepsake." She winked at Pascal.

"We've got all the supplies," Roberto told them. "And we should go before the sunlight fades." He clapped his hands and then rubbed them together. "This is going to be *fantastic!*"

"I can't wait!" Rapunzel said.

Her first art lesson was about to begin!

Chapter Four

*M*aximus looked up as the door to the art shop swung open. Rapunzel rushed over and threw her arms around the horse's thick neck.

"We're off to the meadow for an art lesson!" she sang out happily.

Maximus swatted his tail. He wasn't sure why Rapunzel was so happy, but he was glad to see her smiling.

The shop door's bell jingled again, and Flynn and Pascal walked out, arms piled high with art supplies. Pascal had a box of paintbrushes that was bigger than his whole body! Roberto stopped and flipped a sign on the door that read GONE PAINTING! and then locked up the shop. "Follow me," he said with a huge grin.

"I'm sure there will be some fresh meadow grass for you to munch while we paint," Rapunzel said, encouraging Maximus to follow.

Maximus tilted his head. That carrot had been good, but a meadow filled with sweet, green grass sounded delicious. He wouldn't let that distract him from keeping an eye on Flynn, though. He trailed after Rapunzel and the others.

"It's not that far out of town," Roberto told them. "There's a shortcut here behind the shop."

They followed Roberto to a steep stone stairway behind the store. Getting down the steps was tricky for Maximus, but he kept up.

"How much farther?" Flynn asked. His arms were beginning to hurt, and he was having trouble seeing over the wide load he was carrying. Plus, Rapunzel had just handed him Pascal's paintbrush box.

"Just around the bend," Roberto called over his shoulder.

Rapunzel skipped alongside Flynn. If he hadn't climbed up to her tower, none of this would be happening. She looked over at him. "I've decided I'm going to paint you first,"

she said, smiling mischievously. "I want to give you a gift."

"Thanks," Flynn said, trying to balance the easels.

Pascal scowled. After all their years together, Rapunzel was going to paint Flynn first?

"Just up ahead," Roberto shouted. "Right over this hill."

"A hill?" Flynn moaned. He wasn't sure how much farther he could go.

Rapunzel ran ahead. She was too excited to walk. As she came up over the hill, she gasped. She felt as if she were standing in one of Roberto's paintings! The meadow was in full bloom.

"Wow," she said. She spun around to

take in the whole scene. Then she closed her eyes with her face up to the sun, breathing in the fresh air. She wiggled her toes in the long meadow grass.

"Ah. You like it here?" Roberto said when he caught up to her.

"No, I *love* it here!" she exclaimed. "This is a beautiful place. The colors are spectacular."

"Let's get started," Roberto said. He took the easels from Flynn and set each of them up with a canvas. "Nothing like a blank canvas," he said. He wiped his brow with a handkerchief. "So many possibilities . . ."

Rapunzel took the box of brushes from Pascal and then set up her palette of paint.

"There are different kinds of paintings,"

Roberto said. "There are landscapes that show the scenery around you. You could do a portrait of someone or a still life that showcases fruits or flowers."

Pascal and Flynn both started to yawn, and Maximus put his head down to munch on some sweet meadow grass. But Rapunzel listened to every word Roberto said. She didn't want to miss anything about her first art lesson.

"You need to find your passion," Roberto said. He pointed to the mountains. "Is it the land or something else that you want to paint?"

"I want to paint everything!" Rapunzel exclaimed.

"One canvas at a time," Roberto said,

laughing. "Why not start with a simple landscape?"

Rapunzel dipped her brush into the green paint. She had spent hours gazing out her tower window at the forest. She had already done many paintings of her tower view. Working quickly, she moved her brush across the canvas. A gentle breeze was blowing, and Rapunzel was glad that her long hair was still braided. She wouldn't have wanted it to get in the way of her artwork!

When she was finally satisfied with her painting, Rapunzel turned the canvas around to show Roberto.

"Bravo!" he cried. "Very nice. I love how you painted the trees and the sun. Perhaps you could add some shadows here and over here."

"Thank you," Rapunzel said. After she'd finished, she looked up and saw Pascal and Flynn asleep in the grass. Even Maximus was dozing off. She sighed. Not everyone was as interested in the scenery and painting.

"Let's focus on a portrait now," Roberto said.

With that, Pascal's eyes opened. This was his cue. He sprang up from the grass and watched as Rapunzel set up her easel. But she was only looking at Flynn!

"Flynn," Rapunzel said gently. When he did not move, she grinned at Pascal. Then she moved closer to Flynn's ear and screamed, *"Waaaaake up!"*

Flynn jumped. "Let me go!" he screamed, opening his eyes. "I'm innocent!" To his surprise, the palace guards were not chasing him. He grinned sheepishly. Then he narrowed his eyes at Rapunzel. "I'll remember that."

"You'll have to sit over there on that rock," Rapunzel told him. "The light is perfect there."

"On the rock?" Flynn said, wrinkling his nose. "The cold, hard rock?" Rapunzel scowled and pointed at the rock. "Okay, okay," he said, remembering the frying pan.

Pascal climbed up on the rock as well. But the gray color didn't suit him. He wanted to stand out more, so he changed his skin to a bright green color. The sun was hitting him right in the eye so he jumped to the grass. But if he were green in the grass, Rapunzel wouldn't be able to see him. Quickly, he changed to a deep red.

"Pascal!" Rapunzel scolded. "If you keep

changing colors and positions I can't paint Flynn's portrait properly."

Pascal hung his head. *Flynn's* painting? Wasn't Pascal going to be in it? He curled his lip and scooted off behind a tree to sulk.

Rapunzel put some more paint on her palette and looked up. "Flynn, what are you doing?" she asked.

Flynn was frantically moving his arms around his head. "I'll get that little pest," he grumbled. He was trying to swat a fly that was buzzing above him.

"I can't paint you when you're moving all around," Rapunzel said. "Do you think you could manage to sit still?"

Maximus neighed and gave Flynn a stern look. He wondered if Flynn could sit still long enough for Rapunzel to paint him. It didn't seem likely.

"The hardest stroke is always the first one," Roberto said. He took his handkerchief out and patted his forehead. "You need to capture the moment for the portrait to be truly great."

Rapunzel wanted this painting to be great! She was determined. Carefully, she mixed the brown paint with some golden highlights and began with Flynn's hair. She was enjoying working in the fresh air. Rapunzel had never thought about how sunlight could change her paintings. When she looked up to check the length of Flynn's hair, she saw that he was fast asleep again.

The pesky fly was sitting on top of his

nose, and his mouth was wide open. Suddenly, Flynn began snoring loudly.

Rapunzel put her hand to her mouth to stifle her laughter. She didn't want to wake Flynn—at least not yet!

She dipped her brush in some black paint and drew a little fly on Flynn's nose. She tried not to laugh as she painted.

What a funny portrait this will be, she thought. Roberto had said to capture the moment. That was exactly what she was going to do!

Chapter Five

"Oh, my dear!" Roberto gushed. "This painting looks magnificent!"

Rapunzel loved hearing Roberto's praise. She squealed with delight and woke up her sleeping friend.

"Not guilty!" Flynn shouted as he leaped up from the rock.

Rapunzel began laughing. "Flynn, you fell asleep. Again."

Rubbing his eyes, Flynn stood up and looked around. "Huh, must be all this fresh air. At least you didn't yell at me this time," he said, rubbing his sore ear. He walked over to Rapunzel and looked at the canvas. A smile spread across his face. Rapunzel had painted him with his mouth hanging open and a fly on his nose.

"Looks just like you," Roberto said, coming up to him.

"I was just capturing the moment," Rapunzel said with a smile. "And I made sure you didn't swallow the fly," she added.

Flynn had to laugh. The painting was well done. He bowed to Rapunzel. "Guess I deserved that," he said. "At least you got my nose right!"

Rapunzel reached down for another canvas. "I want to keep painting," she said. "Roberto, this is wonderful. I love being out here, and you were right about the light. I am having a great time."

She looked over and saw Maximus. His coat was shimmering in the sun. Rapunzel picked up her brush and started to paint. Flynn came over and stood next to her.

"Maybe you'd like to try to paint now," Roberto said to Flynn.

Flynn laughed. "I *am* quite an amazing guy, but painting isn't one of my talents," he said.

"He's much better at napping," Rapunzel said, giggling.

Maximus looked up from grazing and

snorted, glad that Rapunzel had been distracted from painting him.

But Rapunzel was determined. She mixed paints until she got Maximus's color just right.

"You know, we should be heading back," Flynn said. He was pacing behind Rapunzel as she worked. "It's getting late."

Rapunzel didn't want to leave, but she knew that soon the sun would set. Then, the lanterns would launch over the palace. Rapunzel couldn't miss that.

"Pascal!" Rapunzel called. "I have the boxes for you to carry."

There was no answer.

She looked around and frowned when she didn't see her colorful pet. "Where'd he go?"

She turned to Roberto and Flynn. "Have you seen Pascal?"

"No, I haven't seen him," Flynn said. He was busy packing up. He shook his head. "He was sitting behind that tree before," Roberto said. But the chameleon wasn't there.

"Did you see him, Maximus?" Flynn walked over to the horse, who had a mouth full of grass.

Maximus snorted and shook his head.

Rapunzel got down on her hands and knees to look for the chameleon. "Come out, Pascal," she called. "Please?"

There was no sign of him. Rapunzel was getting nervous. She sat down on the large rock. "Maybe he's lost? He hasn't been out of our tower much." Tears came to her eyes

as she thought of the little chameleon alone in the meadow. No doubt he would be very scared.

"Pascal!" Flynn shouted. "We're leaving!"

"We are not going to leave without him," Rapunzel said. "He's my friend."

"Maybe he went over to the stream?"

Roberto suggested. Rapunzel lifted her skirt and raced over to the water. She scanned the riverbank, but she didn't see any sign of her pet. Flynn joined her, but he couldn't find Pascal either.

"Pascal can get jealous," she told Flynn. "And when he gets green with envy, he can be very difficult to find."

"Especially in a very green meadow," Flynn added.

"Well, let's split up and see if we can spot him," Rapunzel said. She knew that seeing the lanterns that night wouldn't be nearly as special if Pascal wasn't by her side. She looked up at the sun sinking in the sky. They just had to find him—and fast!

Chapter Six

$\mathcal{A}$s the sun moved lower and lower in the sky, Rapunzel, Flynn, and Roberto searched the meadow. It would be hard enough to find a chameleon in a meadow, but a chameleon who didn't want to be found would be next to impossible.

"Pascal is good at hiding," she said. "One time in the tower, he got so mad at me that he stayed hidden for a whole day."

"That's quite a skill," Flynn said, thinking about the people who were after him. If only he could master hiding . . .

"Please," Rapunzel said to Roberto and Flynn. She put her hands together. "Let's keep looking a little more. I don't think Pascal can be too far."

The search went on. Even Maximus helped. He hung his head low to the ground and sniffed around.

Flynn was sure he had solved the mystery when he squatted down to check under a bush. He thought he had found the sneaky color-changing fellow, but instead a squirrel flew out of the bush in a huff.

Rapunzel kept on checking under trees and bushes. She knew in her heart that

Pascal was still nearby. If only she could spot him. But finding Pascal in this meadow was like finding a tiny barrette in her hair!

Roberto took a rest and leaned against a tree. "Rapunzel, I don't think your frog wants us to find him," he said.

"He's a chameleon," she told him. She sunk down to the ground. "I don't think that he'd leave without saying good-bye." Rapunzel's eyes filled with tears. "He's my best friend." She sniffed a little and put her head in her hands. "He must be very angry at me for something. . . ." Her voice trailed off as she started to sob.

Roberto and Flynn each held out handkerchiefs. Flynn presented his with a flourish, but Rapunzel noticed that it was embroidered with someone else's initials. Flynn smiled sheepishly. "I may have found it drying on a clothesline."

Rapunzel took Roberto's handkerchief.

"Oh, dear," Roberto said, full of sympathy. "This is all very unfortunate."

"Pascal and I have had some great times together," Rapunzel continued. She stopped and blew her nose. She looked up at Roberto and sniffled. "I never would have survived all those long days in the tower without him. He has been a true friend."

Suddenly, there was some rustling in the bush behind Rapunzel. In a flash, a pale green Pascal leaped out of the shrub. He landed right in her lap.

"Pascal!" Rapunzel gasped. She scooped him up and gave him a kiss on his forehead.

Pascal turned a bright red and nuzzled Rapunzel's cheek.

"Oh, I'm so happy that you came back," she told him. "What would I do without you?"

Rolling his eyes, Pascal acted out painting and pointed to Flynn and Maximus. He was showing Rapunzel how she had looked when she was painting earlier.

At that moment, Rapunzel understood what had happened. "Were you jealous because I was painting Flynn and Max?" She stroked Pascal's head. "Silly chameleon, you have no reason to worry. As I just said, you are my best friend."

"No doubt he heard that," Flynn said. "We all did."

"Pascal," Rapunzel said, "I'm sorry if I hurt your feelings." She scratched behind Pascal's red ear. "Any painting with you in it would be a true treasure."

"I hate to break up this love fest, Blondie,"

Flynn said. "But we should be heading back to town."

Rapunzel saw that the sun was nearly behind the mountains. "Yes, we need to get going," she agreed.

"Wait one minute," Roberto begged. "I have just one more detail." Rapunzel had not noticed that Roberto had been painting the whole time she was talking to Pascal. She walked over to take a peek at what he had done.

On his canvas was a beautiful portrait of Rapunzel and Pascal!

Rapunzel beamed with delight. "Roberto, this is gorgeous."

"And it is my gift to you and Pascal," he said, grinning. "The name of this painting is

Two Good Friends in the Meadow. I hope you will hang this in your tower. I would love it if you took it home to remember our time together today."

Rapunzel picked up the canvas. The strong, warm colors of the sunset made a beautiful backdrop. "Careful," Roberto warned. "The paint is still wet!"

"Oh, I know the perfect spot for this at home," Rapunzel told Roberto. "Thank you so much. You have been so kind." She handed the painting to Flynn and reached out and gave Roberto a big hug. "This is the nicest gift I've ever gotten," she said. "We will treasure it forever."

Pascal put his hands on his heart and bowed. He, too, wanted to thank the painter.

Roberto had painted Pascal in a blend of colors so he looked extracolorful.

Roberto flashed a huge smile and picked up the boxes of brushes and paints.

"Let's head back to town," Flynn said.

"Yes, let's head back to the village," Rapunzel said. "Together!"

Chapter Seven

$\mathcal{R}$apunzel sank into a chair in Roberto's art shop. Pascal was perched on her shoulder. Flynn was putting Rapunzel's paintings up around the store.

"I'll just be one minute," Roberto called from the back room. "Hot tea is so nice after an afternoon of painting."

"Thank you," Rapunzel called back. "You have already been so kind." She looked at her paintings from the meadow, put her feet up, and sighed. What a fantastic afternoon! she thought.

"Not bad for a day's work," Flynn said as he hung up Rapunzel's last painting.

"Thank you," she replied.

"Blondie, I can't believe how many paintings you did today," Flynn said, smiling at her.

"That's because I did most of them while you were asleep," Rapunzel replied, giggling.

"Very funny," Flynn said to her. "You know, these adventure days are tiring."

Pascal put his head down on Rapunzel's shoulder. He agreed with Flynn. He was exhausted. All that color changing and hiding in the meadow had made him very sleepy.

Just then, the bell on the store's door jingled. An older woman entered the shop. She was dressed in fancy clothes and held a large jeweled bag. "Look at all these gorgeous paintings!" she exclaimed. She slowly walked around, admiring Rapunzel's work. "These weren't done by Roberto," the woman said.

Flynn stepped forward. "No," he said. "An artist was visiting. She has a great gift." He looked over at Rapunzel and winked.

The woman lifted the eyeglasses that were dangling from a jeweled string around her neck. She perched them on the edge of her nose. Leaning in close, she peered at the painting of Maximus.

Rapunzel looked over at Flynn. She held

her breath. She wasn't sure what the woman was doing.

"This horse is perfect," the woman said. She backed up from the painting and tilted her head. "The brushstrokes are wonderful, and I love the choice of colors for the background." She looked up at Rapunzel. "Is this the horse I saw outside?"

"Yes, it is the same horse," Rapunzel replied. "His name is Maximus."

"Extraordinary work," the woman said, staring at the painting. After a long moment, she turned back to face Rapunzel. "I'm Madame Devina. Do you work here?"

Rapunzel wanted to hide behind her long hair, but it was still securely fastened in her braid. "Well, no," she said bravely.

"Who is the artist? I need to know," Madame Devina demanded.

Rapunzel stood up. "My name is Rapunzel. I painted this piece."

"My word!" Madame Devina said. She took off her glasses and looked Rapunzel up and down. "You *do* have a great gift, my dear. I need to have this painting in my home. I am quite fond of horses, and this particular painting captures the spirit of this horse beautifully."

The bag on Madame Devina's shoulder wiggled, and a tiny, furry head popped up. The cat inside pushed its head out of the hole on the side of the bag.

Pascal was the first one to notice the cat. He jumped up from a chair to a window ledge. He didn't like that twitching pink nose!

The cat saw Pascal and shot out of the bag. The minute the cat saw something moving, she wanted to follow it.

Pascal hopped from the windowsill to a

table to the window seat in the front of the store. Rapunzel turned her head quickly to see what was happening. That sent her long braid flying out, and it whipped Madame Devina in the head. The poor woman was knocked backward into a chair.

Roberto walked in holding a tray of cups and a teapot. The tray rattled as the cat scurried by, surprising him. "What is going on here?" he asked.

"Oh, my heavens!" the woman exclaimed. She held her hand to her heart. "What happened?"

"We've got an old-fashioned chase on our hands," Flynn said, eyeing Pascal. He knew how the little guy felt. Being chased all the time was exhausting. He put up his hand for

Pascal to jump down from the high ledge.

"Buttercup!" Madame Devina yelled. "You stop that nonsense right this minute." She wagged her finger at the golden-colored cat. "Get back in your carrier and stop making a nuisance of yourself."

Pascal landed in Flynn's hand and smirked as Buttercup headed back to Madame Devina's bag with his tail between his legs.

After the cat was in the bag, Madame Devina turned back to Rapunzel. "I am sorry about that. I hope your little friend is all right. Buttercup doesn't mean any harm."

Rapunzel smiled. She looked at Buttercup. Maybe he wanted to get out for an adventure, too. Everyone deserved an adventure day now and again.

"No harm done," she said sweetly. She walked over to the horse painting and took it down. "If you really like this painting, then you should have it."

"Wait," Roberto said. "Artists don't give art away—they sell it, my dear!"

Madame Devina smiled. "Yes, and I would love to buy this painting. And if you are like most artists, I'm sure you could use the money."

Rapunzel's mouth fell open. She couldn't believe someone wanted to buy one of her paintings! She wasn't quite sure what to say. What would she do with the money? She looked to Roberto for the answer as she hugged her braid against her chest. This was all too good to be true.

Chapter Eight

$\mathcal{M}$adame Devina walked over to Rapunzel. She placed her bag on the table and then reached out to hold Rapunzel's hands.

"You have a wonderful talent, young lady," she said. Then she peered at Rapunzel's thick blond braid. "And an extraordinary amount of hair!"

"Thank you," Rapunzel said. She touched

a few of the flowers in her hair to make sure the braid was secure. "Painting for other people is very new to me."

"Well," said Madame Devina, smiling, "then we should have a party to celebrate!"

Roberto clapped his hands together. "Excellent idea, Madame," he added. "We can have an official showing of your artwork. Come, let's decorate!"

"But . . . I have to get going," Rapunzel started to say. "I don't have much time."

Roberto and Madame Devina were already scurrying around the shop. They couldn't be stopped!

"I'll go tell Katherine and Margot down the street," Madame Devina said. "They will be sure to get everyone here for a party."

"And I'll tell George to send over some pastries," Roberto offered. "A party needs some special treats!"

Rapunzel looked over at Flynn. He shrugged. He didn't mind—they would still make it to the lanterns, if they were fast.

In just a few moments, the store had become a party scene, complete with decorations, food, and people!

"A painter's first sale is memorable," Roberto said to Rapunzel. He handed her a glass of lemonade and a cream puff drizzled with chocolate. "Now you are a true working artist. Congratulations!"

"Thank you," Rapunzel said. She took a bite of the cream puff. She had never tasted anything so delicious. Having a party was more fun than she had ever imagined.

"Flynn, this is fantastic," Rapunzel whispered to him.

Flynn and Pascal were standing next to the food table. Flynn licked his fingers.

"These cream puffs are good," he said. "Roberto knows how to throw a party."

"I've never been to an actual party," Rapunzel admitted. She looked down at her feet.

"No big birthday parties in the tower?" Flynn asked, raising his eyebrows.

"No," Rapunzel said sadly. "Usually it's just Mother Gothel, Pascal, and me."

Pascal lifted his head and nodded. Then he reached out and shoved another cream puff into his mouth. He rubbed his tummy and smiled.

"And this is the artist," Roberto said, pulling Rapunzel over to meet a friend. "Rapunzel, this is the bookstore owner. He wants to buy one of your paintings."

Rapunzel smiled so wide that her cheeks

began to hurt! She still couldn't believe that people liked her work.

"This is my most successful art show!" Roberto exclaimed happily. "We've sold all of your paintings." He opened his cash box to reveal many gold coins. He handed it to Rapunzel. "This is all well deserved."

"Please, take this money," Rapunzel said. She pushed the box toward Roberto. "It's for the art lesson and so much more. Today was a perfect day."

Flynn's eyes widened. "You know, maybe I should hold on to the money for you. I could go buy Roberto a gift . . . and still have some left over."

Pascal turned red. He stamped his foot.

Rapunzel shook her head.

"I want him to be able to go back home." Rapunzel continued, turning to Roberto, "You need to paint the seaside. Please, take this money."

Roberto was overwhelmed. "You are making my dreams come true," he said. He burst into tears.

"Oh, why are you crying?" Rapunzel asked. She had not meant to upset him. "Did I do something wrong?"

"Those are tears of joy," Madame Devina said, handing Roberto a handkerchief. "Rapunzel, you have made Roberto very, very happy."

"And what about your dream, Rapunzel?" Flynn asked softly. He glanced out the window at the darkening sky. He knew that soon the lanterns would be launched.

Roberto walked over to a large cabinet in the back of the shop. He opened the doors and pulled a shiny tin box from a shelf. "I want you to have this set of paintbrushes," he said to Rapunzel.

"Oh, Roberto." Rapunzel gushed. "You have already given me so many gifts." She opened up the box and saw the rows of brushes in all different sizes. The handles were all bright red and the tops were shiny silver. The brushes had never been used. "Wow," she whispered. She held up one to show Flynn.

"I was saving these brushes for a special project," Roberto said. "I would like it if you'd take them."

Rapunzel reached out and gave Roberto a tight hug. "I will never forget you. Or this day! And I will treasure these brushes forever."

"Will you come visit me again?" Roberto asked.

"Yes, please come back again," Madame Devina said.

Rapunzel looked down at the floor. This adventure day was a big step for her. She wasn't sure what Mother Gothel would say about art lessons with Roberto. If only Mother Gothel could meet Roberto and see how kind he was. And how he and Madame Devina had thrown such a lovely party for her.

"If Rapunzel is back in town, she'll swing by," Flynn said.

Rapunzel smiled at him gratefully. He took her hand and led her to the door.

Rapunzel, Flynn, and Pascal headed out. Maximus was waiting for them to go down to the canal.

Rapunzel had set out with Flynn to see the lanterns. She hadn't hoped for anything else along the way. Now she had sold her paintings, like a true artist . . . and made some new friends.

She looked at Flynn. Life had been full of surprises since he'd shown up at the tower.

"Race you to the canal." Flynn took off running.

Rapunzel looked at Maximus and grinned. She hopped up into the saddle with Pascal and trotted up to Flynn. "You might want to

rethink that plan. On second thought, this would make a funny painting."

She clicked her heels, and Maximus bolted forward.

Flynn chased after them. Somehow he didn't think this would be the last time Rapunzel surprised him.

Don't miss these enchanting Disney Princess chapter books!

Aurora
The
Perfect
Party

*B*eing a princess is a dream come true. But sometimes, Aurora misses the days she spent in the woodcutter's cottage with the three good fairies. The princess decides to throw them a surprise party. She'll gather their favorite items from the cottage and invite all their forest friends to the castle! But can the princess keep her perfect party plans a secret from the fairies before the big day?

Jasmine
The Missing Coin

*A*laddin's birthday is just around the corner. Jasmine wants to find him the perfect gift, so she sets off on the Magic Carpet with Rajah the tiger. She is determined to track down a camel coin Aladdin needs for his rare-coin collection. It's smooth sailing until the Magic Carpet suddenly stops, stranding Jasmine and Rajah in the desert! Will they find the special coin and make it back to the palace in time for Aladdin's birthday celebration?

Tiana
The Grand Opening

*T*iana has always dreamed of having her own restaurant, and now her dream is about to come true. The grand opening is just around the corner, and all of Tiana's friends and family will be there, along with a famous food critic! But suddenly everything starts to go wrong. Her bandleader Louis loses his prized trumpet. Then the power goes out after the guests arrive. Will the princess be able to fix things in time, or will her big night be a royal disaster?